This book belongs to

_____

THE TALE OF
MRS. TIGGY-WINKLE

BEATRIX POTTER
ILLUSTRATED BY
ALLEN ATKINSON

AN ARIEL BOOK

BANTAM BOOKS
TORONTO   NEW YORK   LONDON   SYDNEY   AUCKLAND

THE TALE OF MRS. TIGGY-WINKLE
A Bantam Book
April 1983

Design: Iris Bass
Editorial Director: Ron Buehl
Senior Editor: Lu Ann Walther
Production: Hal Hochvert
Art Direction: Armand Eisen

ISBN 0-553-15204-1

Bantam Books are published by Bantam Books, Inc. Its trademark, consisting of the words "Bantam Books" and the portrayal of a rooster, is Registered in U.S. Patent and Trademark Office and in other countries. Marca Registrada. Bantam Books, Inc., 666 Fifth Avenue, New York, New York 10103

Printing and binding by
Printer, industria gráfica S.A   Provenza, 388   Barcelona-25
Depósito legal B. 41011-1983
PRINTED IN SPAIN
0 9 8 7 6 5 4

The art is dedicated
to my grandmother,
Mrs. Mary Cable

ONCE UPON A TIME there was a little girl called Lucie, who lived at a farm called Little-town.

THE TALE OF MRS. TIGGY-WINKLE

She was a good little girl—
only she was always losing her
pocket-handkerchiefs!

THE TALE OF MRS. TIGGY-WINKLE

One day little Lucie came into the farm-yard crying—oh, she did cry so! "I've lost my pocket-handkin! Three handkins and a pinny! Have *you* seen them, Tabby Kitten?"

The Kitten went on washing her white paws; so Lucie asked a speckled hen—

THE TALE OF MRS. TIGGY-WINKLE

THE TALE OF MRS. TIGGY-WINKLE

"Sally Henny-penny, have *you* found three pocket-handkins?"

But the speckled hen ran into a barn, clucking—

"I go barefoot,

barefoot,

barefoot!"

THE TALE OF MRS. TIGGY-WINKLE

And then Lucie asked Cock Robin
sitting on a twig.

Cock Robin looked sideways at Lucie
with his bright black eye, and he flew
over a stile and away.

THE TALE OF MRS. TIGGY-WINKLE

THE TALE OF MRS. TIGGY-WINKLE

Lucie climbed upon the stile and looked up at the hill behind Little-town—a hill that goes up—up—into the clouds as though it had no top!

And a great way up the hill-side she thought she saw some white things spread upon the grass.

THE TALE OF MRS. TIGGY-WINKLE

Lucie scrambled up the hill as fast as her stout legs would carry her; she ran along a steep path-way—up and up—until Little-town was right away down below—she could have dropped a pebble down the chimney!

THE TALE OF MRS. TIGGY-WINKLE

THE TALE OF MRS. TIGGY-WINKLE

19

Presently she came to a spring, bubbling out from the hill-side.

Some one had stood a tin can upon a stone to catch the water—but the water was already running over, for the can was no bigger than an egg-cup!

THE TALE OF MRS. TIGGY-WINKLE

And where the
sand upon the path
was wet—there were
foot-marks of a
very small person.

Lucie ran on, and on.

The path ended under a big rock. The grass was short and green, and there were clothes-props cut from bracken stems, with lines of plaited rushes, and a heap of tiny clothes pins—but no pocket-handkerchiefs!

THE TALE OF MRS. TIGGY-WINKLE

THE TALE OF MRS. TIGGY-WINKLE

But there was something else—a door! straight into the hill; and inside it some one was singing—

> "Lily-white and clean, oh!
> With little frills between, oh!

Smooth and hot—red rusty spot
Never here be seen, oh!"

Lucie, knocked—once—twice, and interrupted the song. A little frightened voice called out "Who's that?"

Lucie opened the door: and what do you think there was inside the hill?—a nice clean kitchen with a flagged floor and wooden beams—just like any other farm kitchen. Only the ceiling was so low that Lucie's head nearly touched it; and the pots and pans were small, and so was everything there.

THE TALE OF MRS. TIGGY-WINKLE

THE TALE OF MRS. TIGGY-WINKLE

THE TALE OF MRS. TIGGY-WINKLE

There was a nice hot singey smell; and at the table, with an iron in her hand stood a very stout short person staring anxiously at Lucie.

Her print gown was tucked up, and she was wearing a large apron over her striped petticoat. Her little black nose went sniffle, sniffle, snuffle, and her eyes went twinkle, twinkle; and underneath her cap—where Lucie had yellow curls—that little person had PRICKLES!

THE TALE OF MRS. TIGGY-WINKLE

"Who are you?" said Lucie. "Have you seen my pocket-handkins?"

The little person made a bob-curtsey —"Oh, yes, if you please'm; my name is Mrs. Tiggy-winkle; oh, yes if you please'm, I'm an excellent clear-starcher!" And she took something out of a clothes-basket, and spread it on the ironing-blanket.

"What's that thing?" said Lucie—"that's not my pocket-handkin?"

"Oh no, if you please'm; that's a little scarlet waist-coat belonging to Cock Robin!"

And she ironed it and folded it, and put it on one side.

Then she took something else off a clothes-horse—"That isn't my pinny?" said Lucie.

THE TALE OF MRS. TIGGY-WINKLE

THE TALE OF MRS. TIGGY-WINKLE

"Oh no, if you please'm; that's a damask table-cloth belonging to Jenny Wren; look how it's stained with currant wine! It's very bad to wash!" said Mrs. Tiggy-winkle.

Mrs. Tiggy-winkle's nose went sniffle, sniffle, snuffle, and her eyes went twinkle, twinkle; and she fetched another hot iron from the fire.

"There's one of my pocket-handkins!"
cried Lucie—"and there's my pinny!"

Mrs. Tiggy-winkle ironed it, and
goffered it, and shook out the frills.

"Oh that *is* lovely!" said Lucie.

THE TALE OF MRS. TIGGY-WINKLE

THE TALE OF MRS. TIGGY-WINKLE

"And what are those long yellow things with fingers like gloves?"

"Oh, that's a pair of stockings belonging to Sally Henny-penny—look how she's worn the heels out with scratching in the yard! She'll very soon go barefoot!" said Mrs. Tiggy-winkle.

"Why, there's another handkersniff—
but it isn't mine; it's red?"

"Oh no, if you please'm; that one
belongs to old Mrs. Rabbit; and it *did* so
smell of onions! I've had to wash it
separately, I can't get out the smell."

"There's another one of mine," said
Lucie.

"What are those funny little white things?"

"That's a pair of mittens belonging to Tabby Kitten; I only have to iron them; she washes them herself."

"There's my last pocket-handkin!" said Lucie.

"And what are you dipping into the basin of starch?"

THE TALE OF MRS. TIGGY-WINKLE

"They're little dicky shirt-fronts belonging to Tom Tit-mouse—most terrible particular!" said Mrs. Tiggy-winkle. "Now I've finished my ironing; I'm going to air some clothes."

THE TALE OF MRS. TIGGY-WINKLE

"What are these dear soft fluffy things?" said Lucie.

"Oh those are woolly coats belonging to the little lambs at Skelghyl."

"Will their jackets take off?" asked Lucie.

THE TALE OF MRS. TIGGY-WINKLE

"Oh yes, if you please'm; look at the sheep-mark on the shoulder. And here's one marked for Gatesgarth, and three that come from Little-town. They're *always* marked at washing!" said Mrs. Tiggy-winkle.

THE TALE OF MRS. TIGGY-WINKLE

And she hung up all sorts and sizes of clothes—small brown coats of mice; and one velvety black moleskin waist-coat; and a red tailcoat with no tail belonging to Squirrel Nutkin; and a very much

THE TALE OF MRS. TIGGY-WINKLE

shrunk blue jacket belonging to Peter
Rabbit; and a petticoat, not marked, that
had gone lost in the washing—and at
last the basket was empty!

THE TALE OF MRS. TIGGY-WINKLE

THE TALE OF MRS. TIGGY-WINKLE

Then Mrs. Tiggy-winkle made tea—a cup for herself and a cup for Lucie. They sat before the fire on a bench and looked sideways at one another. Mrs. Tiggy-winkle's hand, holding the tea-cup, was very very brown, and very very wrinkly with the soap-suds; and all through her gown and her cap, there were *hair-pins* sticking wrong end out; so that Lucie didn't like to sit too near her.

When they had finished tea, they tied up the clothes in bundles; and Lucie's pocket-handkerchiefs were folded up inside her clean pinny, and fastened with a silver safety-pin.

THE TALE OF MRS. TIGGY-WINKLE

THE TALE OF MRS. TIGGY-WINKLE

THE TALE OF MRS. TIGGY-WINKLE

And then they made up the fire with turf, and came out and locked the door, and hid the key under the door-sill.

Then away down the hill trotted Lucie and Mrs. Tiggy-winkle with the bundles of clothes!

THE TALE OF MRS. TIGGY-WINKLE

All the way down the path little animals came out of the fern to meet them; the very first that they met were Peter Rabbit and Benjamin Bunny!

THE TALE OF MRS. TIGGY-WINKLE

THE TALE OF MRS. TIGGY-WINKLE

And she gave them their nice clean clothes; and all the little animals and birds were so very much obliged to dear Mrs. Tiggy-winkle.

THE TALE OF MRS. TIGGY-WINKLE

So that at the bottom of the hill when they came to the stile, there was nothing left to carry except Lucie's one little bundle.

Lucie scrambled up the stile with the bundle in her hand; and then she turned to say "Good-night," and to thank the washer-woman—

THE TALE OF MRS. TIGGY-WINKLE

But what a *very* odd thing! Mrs. Tiggy-winkle had not waited either for thanks or for the washing bill!

She was running running running up the hill—and where was her white frilled cap? and her shawl? and her gown—and her petticoat?

THE TALE OF MRS. TIGGY-WINKLE

And *how* small she had grown—
and *how* brown—and
covered with
PRICKLES!

THE TALE OF MRS. TIGGY-WINKLE

THE TALE OF MRS. TIGGY-WINKLE

Why! Mrs. Tiggy-winkle was nothing but a HEDGEHOG.

* * * * *

(Now some people say that little Lucie had been asleep upon the stile—but then how could she have found three clean pocket-handkins and a pinny, pinned with a silver safety-pin?

And besides—*I* have seen that door into the back of the hill called Cat Bells—and besides *I* am very well acquainted with dear Mrs. Tiggy-winkle!)

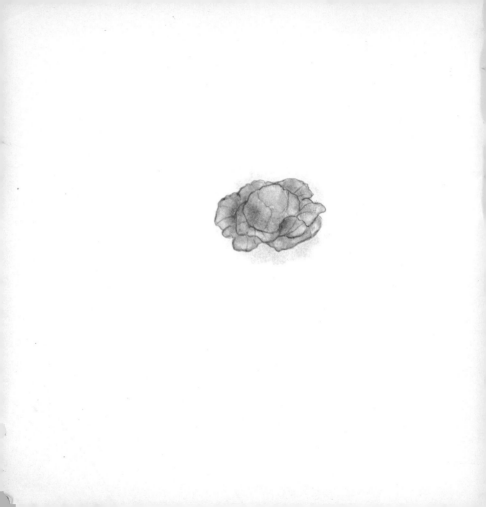